KIDS' SPORTS STORIES

SOCCER DREAMS

by Shawn Pryor

illustrated by Genevieve Kote

PICTURE WINDOW BOOKS
a capstone imprint

Kids' Sports Stories is published by Picture Window Books, an imprint of Capstone.
1710 Roe Crest Drive, North Mankato, Minnesota 56003
www.capstonepub.com

Library of Congress Cataloging-in-Publication Data is available
on the Library of Congress website.
ISBN 978-1-5158-4808-0 (library binding)
ISBN 978-1-5158-5879-9 (paperback)
ISBN 978-1-5158-4809-7 (eBook PDF)

Summary: Wanting to be a striker like her grandpa was, Keisha jumps into soccer practice with both feet and, unfortunately, both hands. She's afraid her habit of catching the ball will end her sports dream, but Coach has a new game plan.

Designer: Ted Williams

Printed in the United States of America.
PA100

TABLE OF CONTENTS

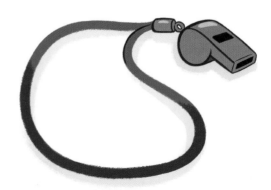

Glossary

 **goal**—the area within which players must put the ball to score

 **goalkeeper**—the player who protects the goal and keeps the other team from scoring

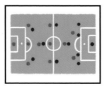 **position**—the part someone plays on a team; each position has a set job to do and needs different skills

 **save**—a move that keeps the other team from scoring

 **striker**—a player whose main job is to score; also called a forward

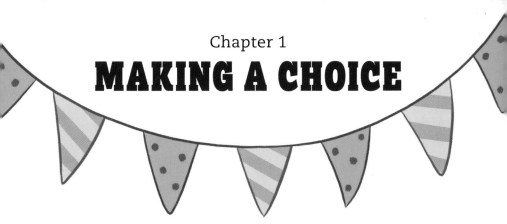

Chapter 1
MAKING A CHOICE

Keisha was at the City Sports Fair with her parents. Kids could sign up for a team sport. There were so many sports to choose from! Keisha wanted to find the right one for her.

Her mother pointed at one of the team tables. "Keisha, would you like to play basketball?" she asked.

"No," Keisha said. "That's not my thing."

Her father pointed at another table. "How about the swim team?" he asked.

Keisha shook her head. "Swimming is fun, but water gets stuck in my ears," she said. "That makes me grumpy."

"So, no swimming," said her father.

Golf was also a no. So were gymnastics and tennis.

Suddenly, Keisha grabbed her mother's hand and pulled. "Mom! Over here! Hurry!" she said.

Keisha and her mom ran down a long row. Her dad followed.

"Slow down, sweetie," Keisha's mom said. "If you want to sign up for track, you just passed by that table!"

Keisha finally stopped. In front of her stood a boy bouncing a soccer ball on his foot. He did all sorts of cool tricks with the ball.

"I want to play soccer!"
Keisha shouted.

Keisha's parents looked at her and grinned. "Really?" they said together.

Keisha smiled. "I watch soccer with Grandpa all the time," she said. "He played striker in college. I want to be a striker and score goals like Grandpa! Sign me up!"

Chapter 2

STRIKING OUT

Keisha and her teammates stood in a circle. They bounced on their toes. Soccer practice was so exciting! Every day they learned something new.

"Today we'll see what position fits you best," Coach said. "Every position on the field is important."

"I want to score a goal!" Keisha said.

"Me too!" said Tyler.

Coach spun the soccer ball in her hands. "First position we're going to try is striker," she said. "Line up!"

Keisha raced to the front of the line.

"Show us what you got, Keisha!" Coach said.

Coach rolled the ball Keisha's way.

Keisha made a booming kick. It hit
the back of the net!

"Nice goal!" Coach said.

The rest of the team took their turns
kicking the ball. After a few minutes,
Coach blew her whistle.

"Now let's see your passing skills," she said. "Find a partner and start passing to each other."

Tyler and Keisha paired up. Tyler kicked the ball. Keisha caught it with her hands.

"You can't catch the ball. You have to stop it with your feet, chest, or head," said Tyler.

Keisha's face felt hot. "Sorry," she said. She rolled the ball back.

"It's OK," Tyler said. "Let's try again."

Tyler kicked the ball to Keisha a second time. She caught it again.

"Sorry," Keisha said.

Coach blew her whistle. "All right, team, let's do some running!" she yelled. "Strikers need to be quick. Line up at midfield!"

The kids lined up. Keisha knew she had to win this race. She had to show Coach she would be a great striker.

"When I blow my whistle, run to the goal line and back," said Coach.

PWEEEEEEET!

The kids took off! Keisha kept up at first. Then she fell behind. Her teammates passed by her.

Keisha finished next to last.

Chapter 3

KEISHA'S A KEEPER

After the race, Coach gave the news to the team. "Tyler, Tina, and Kevin, you're our strikers," she said.

"I am? Awesome!" said Tyler.

"Cool!" said Tina and Kevin.

Keisha walked away with her head down.

"Let's take a short break, everyone," Coach said.

Coach walked over to Keisha. She asked what was wrong.

Keisha wiped away her tears. "I'm not a striker," she said. "I wanted to be like my grandpa."

Coach put her hand on Keisha's shoulder. "Remember what I said earlier?" she asked.

Keisha nodded. "Every position is important," she said.

"Right!" Coach said. "You've got some good skills, Keisha. You're strong, and you can catch the ball really well."

"But we aren't allowed to catch the ball," Keisha said.

"Strikers aren't, but goalkeepers are," Coach said. "They stop the ball from going in the net. Come here. Let's try something."

Coach walked Keisha to the goal. The rest of the team watched.

"OK, Keisha," Coach said. "I'm going to kick the ball. You stop it."

Keisha's stomach twisted and turned. She didn't know if she could do it. Coach kicked. The ball flew toward the goal.

Keisha jumped, reached, and made a diving catch!

"I did it!" she yelled.

"Nice hands, Keisha! Great save!" Tyler said.

One by one, Coach and Keisha's teammates tried to score a goal. Keisha blocked every shot.

"Keisha's amazing!" Kevin said.

"With practice and help from your teammates, Keisha, you'll get even better," Coach said.

Keisha smiled. "Thanks, Coach," she said. "Being a goalkeeper is awesome! I can't wait to tell my grandpa. And I can't wait to play my first game!"

RED LIGHT, GREEN LIGHT

Dribbling is a basic soccer skill that helps you move the ball down the field in a controlled way. To dribble, use the inside or top of your foot and tap the ball. Use both feet and try not to look at them while dribbling. Keep the ball in your control.

Gather a few friends and give this game a try. You'll have fun and build skills too!

What You Need:
- a large grassy area
- a soccer ball for each person

What You Do:
1. Line up your friends shoulder to shoulder. Each person should have a ball at his or her feet.
2. Walk 40 steps away and stop.
3. With your back to your friends, yell "Green light!" At this signal, everyone dribbles toward you.
4. After a couple seconds, yell "Red light!" At this signal, everyone must stop.
5. After you yell, turn around quickly. See if you can catch someone who's still moving. Anyone caught moving must go back to the starting line.
6. Repeat steps 1 through 5 until someone reaches you. Then pick a new person to be "it."

REPLAY IT

Take another look at this illustration. How do you think Keisha felt when Coach kicked the ball toward the net? What do you think Keisha saw and heard?

Now pretend you're Keisha. Write a letter to your grandpa that tells him all about this big moment.

ABOUT THE AUTHOR

Shawn Pryor is the creator and co-author of the graphic novel mystery series Cash & Carrie, co-creator and author of the 2019 GLYPH-nominated football/drama series Force, and author of *Kentucky Kaiju* and *Jake Maddox: Diamond Double Play*. In his free time, he enjoys reading, cooking, listening to streaming music playlists, and talking about why Zack from the Mighty Morphin Power Rangers is the greatest superhero of all time.

ABOUT
THE ILLUSTRATOR

Genevieve Kote is an illustrator whose lively work has appeared in popular magazines such as *American Girl* and *Nickelodeon*, children's books, comics, and newspapers. When she's not illustrating, she enjoys baking and reading at her home in Montreal, Canada. View more of her artwork at genevievekote.com.